Published by Stone Arch Books,
an imprint of Capstone.
1710 Roe Crest Drive
North Mankato, Minnesota 56003
www.capstonepub.com

Library of Congress Cataloging-in-Publication Data is available
on the Library of Congress website.
ISBN: 978-1-4965-8723-7 (library binding)
ISBN: 978-1-4965-9201-9 (paperback)
ISBN: 978-1-4965-8727-5 (eBook PDF)

Summary: After Parademons strike Metropolis, Superman heads to Apokolips to cut off any future attacks. But has the Man of Steel walked right into a trap? Mister Miracle and Big Barda think so, but they can't just leave Earth defenseless while they go warn him. Luckily, Lois Lane and Jimmy Olsen are up for the challenge. Can they help Superman in a bid to spur a rebellion against the almighty ruler of Apokolips?

Designer: Kyle Grenz

Printed and bound in the USA.
PA100

P9-BZH-748

SUPER HEROES

SUPERMAN

AND THE

APOKOLIPS
ATTACK

WRITTEN BY
IVAN COHEN

ILLUSTRATED BY
GREGG SCHIG

SUPERMAN CREATED BY
JERRY SIEGEL AND JOE SHUSTER
BY SPECIAL ARRANGEMENT WITH THE JERRY SI

NEW GODS CREATED BY JACK KIRBY

TABLE OF CONTENTS

Years ago in a distant galaxy, the planet Krypton exploded. Its only survivor was a baby named Kal-El who escaped in a rocket ship. After landing on Earth, he was adopted by the Kents, a kind couple who named him Clark. The boy soon discovered he had extraordinary abilities fueled by the yellow sun of Earth. He chose to use these powers to help others, and so he became the guardian of his new home.

He is . . .

SUPERMAN ™

CHAPTER 1

INVASION FROM BEYOND

PING! PING! PING! PING! PING!

Clark Kent, Lois Lane, and Jimmy Olsen stepped back as the mysterious black machine on the table started pinging. The *Daily Planet's* two star reporters and their photographer had just arrived at the press conference at S.T.A.R. Labs.

The friends had been to the world-famous scientific laboratory many times. They knew it always had interesting technology, but this machine was even more interesting than usual. Although it had been found in Metropolis Harbor, S.T.A.R.'s scientists thought it came from another planet!

"What do you think it is, Miss Lane?" Jimmy asked as he started taking photos.

"I don't know, Jimmy," Lois answered. "But whatever it is, it's going to make the front page of the paper. Did you notice it only started making that pinging noise when we got close?"

Clark, who was actually Superman in disguise, had *definitely* noticed. And he had a strong feeling the timing wasn't an accident.

Clark lifted his glasses slightly and secretly peered at the device with his X-ray vision. While he didn't recognize the box itself, he knew he had seen the type of technology it used before. The device was definitely from Apokolips, the distant planet ruled by the evil Darkseid—a super-villain whose powers rivaled even Superman's!

Darkseid had incredible physical strength and near-invulnerability. He could also fire energy blasts, called Omega Beams, from his eyes. Omega Beams could track an enemy like a missile. They could either destroy their target or send it to other places.

Darkseid was bad enough, but the villain didn't rule over Apokolips's harsh landscape alone. He had superpowered lieutenants who loved to follow his commands. He also had an army of near-mindless creatures called Parademons. These flying, armored soldiers followed Darkseid's every order without question.

Clark set his glasses back down and stepped toward the device again. The moment he did, it lit up with unearthly energies.

BOOM!

Clark knew what that sound meant. Rushing to a nearby window, he watched as a Boom Tube opened in the sky above Metropolis. Boom Tubes were tunnels used to travel great distances through space in an instant. Now a stream of Parademons poured through this one from Apokolips!

"I'd better call the police," said Clark.

"But Clark," Lois exclaimed, "you'll miss the story of the—"

Before Lois could finish her sentence, Clark dashed from the lab and rushed to the rooftop. Instead of calling the police, he ducked behind a large air conditioner. Seconds later he came out wearing his red, blue, and yellow uniform.

"This looks like a job for Superman," the Man of Steel said. Then he flew into the air to face the Parademons darkening the sky.

Hovering above Hob's Bay in Metropolis Harbor, Superman spotted a group of Parademons flying toward Hobsneck Bridge. Their energy weapons glowed as Darkseid's soldiers took aim at the bridge's support cables.

ZAAT! ZAAT!

Flying at full speed, Superman swooped between the energy blasts and the bridge. As the rays bounced harmlessly off of his chest, the hero targeted the Parademons' weapons with his heat vision.

ZAP! KA-BOOM!

The weapons exploded in their hands!

With the Parademons stunned, Superman zipped down to a nearby fishing boat. He grabbed a large net and flew circles around Darkseid's soldiers.

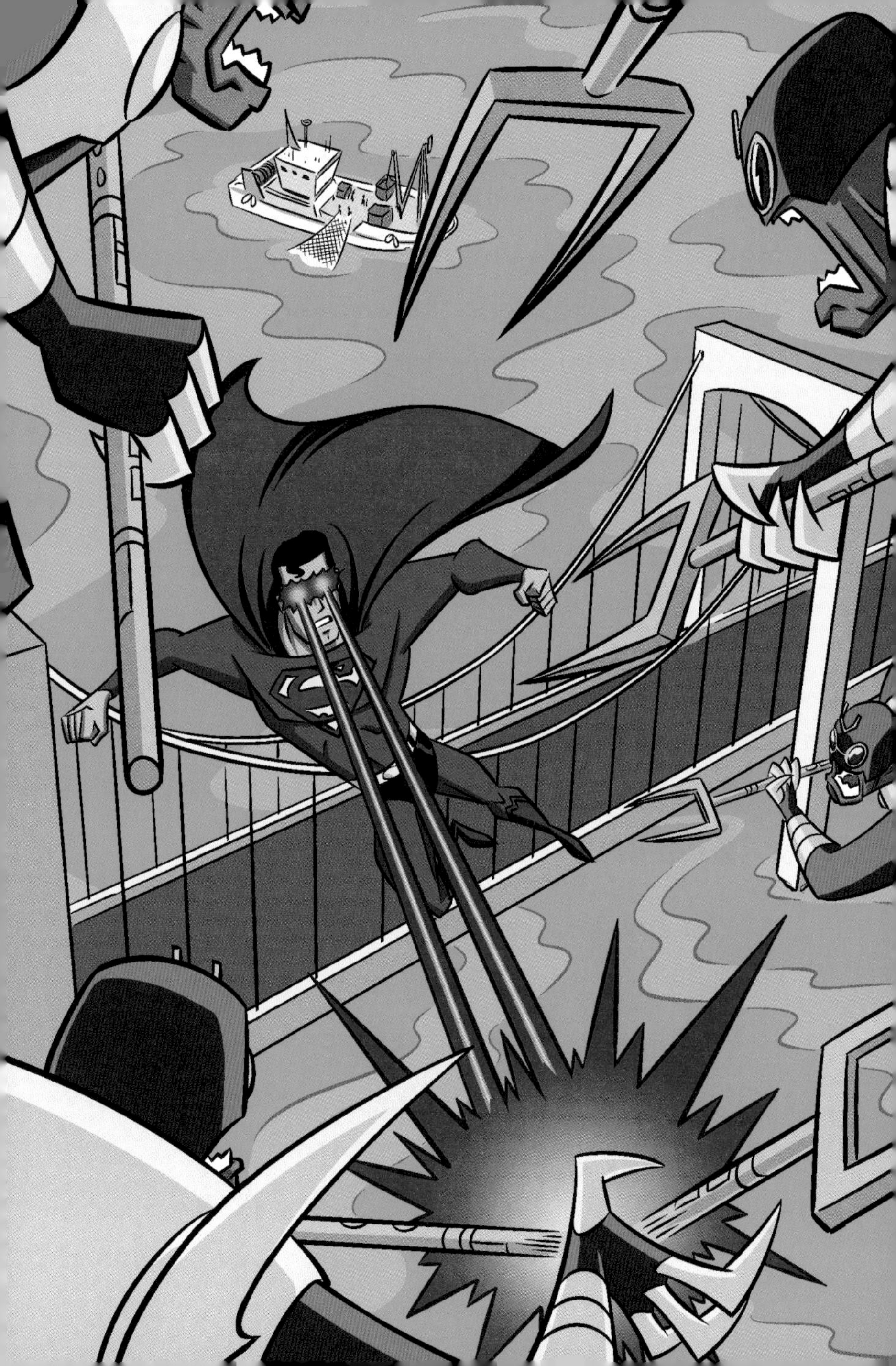

In seconds, the Parademons became tangled in the net. Taking careful aim, Superman hurled the creatures back through the Boom Tube. Along the way, they knocked another wave of troops back to Apokolips.

With one swarm of Parademons down, Superman scanned the sky for more. He quickly spotted another group closing in on an airplane coming in for a landing at the Metropolis airport.

Without wasting a moment, Superman flew straight into the pack of Parademons.

WHACK!

His blow knocked Darkseid's soldiers aside like bowling pins, clearing the plane's path to the runway. As the Parademons tried to regroup, Superman used a tightly aimed burst of super-breath to sweep them back into the Boom Tube.

The Man of Steel looked around and realized his work was far from done. Zooming from one end of Metropolis to the other, he gathered up swarms of Parademons again and again. Then he sent them back through the Boom Tube to Apokolips. But as quickly as he sent one group away, a fresh group would come through.

This isn't working, Superman realized. Although he had cleared the skies of Parademons for the moment, he was also growing tired of this endless battle. *Is there no limit to the number of soldiers Darkseid can send to Metropolis?*

I've got to take the battle to the source, Superman decided. With a burst of speed, he flew back to S.T.A.R. Labs. He swooped through a window and grabbed the device that had opened the Boom Tube.

Meanwhile, Lois and Jimmy stood on the roof of S.T.A.R. Labs. Lois was taking notes on the invasion, while Jimmy snapped photos of the action in every direction.

WHOOSH!

Superman flew past them, ruffling the pages of Lois's notebook!

"What's he doing?" asked Lois, squinting at the red-and-blue blur shooting across the sky.

Jimmy looked through his camera's viewfinder. "He's flying that gadget straight into the Boom Tube!"

As Jimmy captured more photos, Superman disappeared into the tunnel. Seconds later, the Boom Tube blinked and vanished too. The skies over Metropolis became calm once again.

"He did it!" Jimmy shouted. "The Parademons are gone!"

"But so is Superman," a worried Lois replied. "Let's get back downstairs. I've got a few questions for those S.T.A.R. Labs scientists."

As soon as they returned to the lab, Lois marched over to the first scientist she spotted. But before she could ask a question, the door to the lab flew off its hinges!

An unusual couple entered the lab. One was a tall, powerful woman wearing a helmet and body armor. She carried a glowing baton-shaped weapon on her hip. It looked oddly similar to the Parademons' weapons. The other person was an athletic man wearing a colorful red, yellow, and green uniform.

"You're Mister Miracle! The world's greatest escape artist!" Jimmy exclaimed. Then he looked at the woman, who scanned the lab with a soldier's gaze. "And that means *you* must be his wife, Big—"

"Big Barda, yes," she said impatiently. "But there's no time for small talk. We must find Superman!"

"You're too late," Lois replied, looking up at the towering super hero. "Superman flew into the tunnel that released those creatures. But he should be back any minute. You can talk it over with him then—as long as I get the exclusive."

Barda and her husband exchanged worried looks.

"What's going on?" Jimmy asked. "What aren't you telling us?

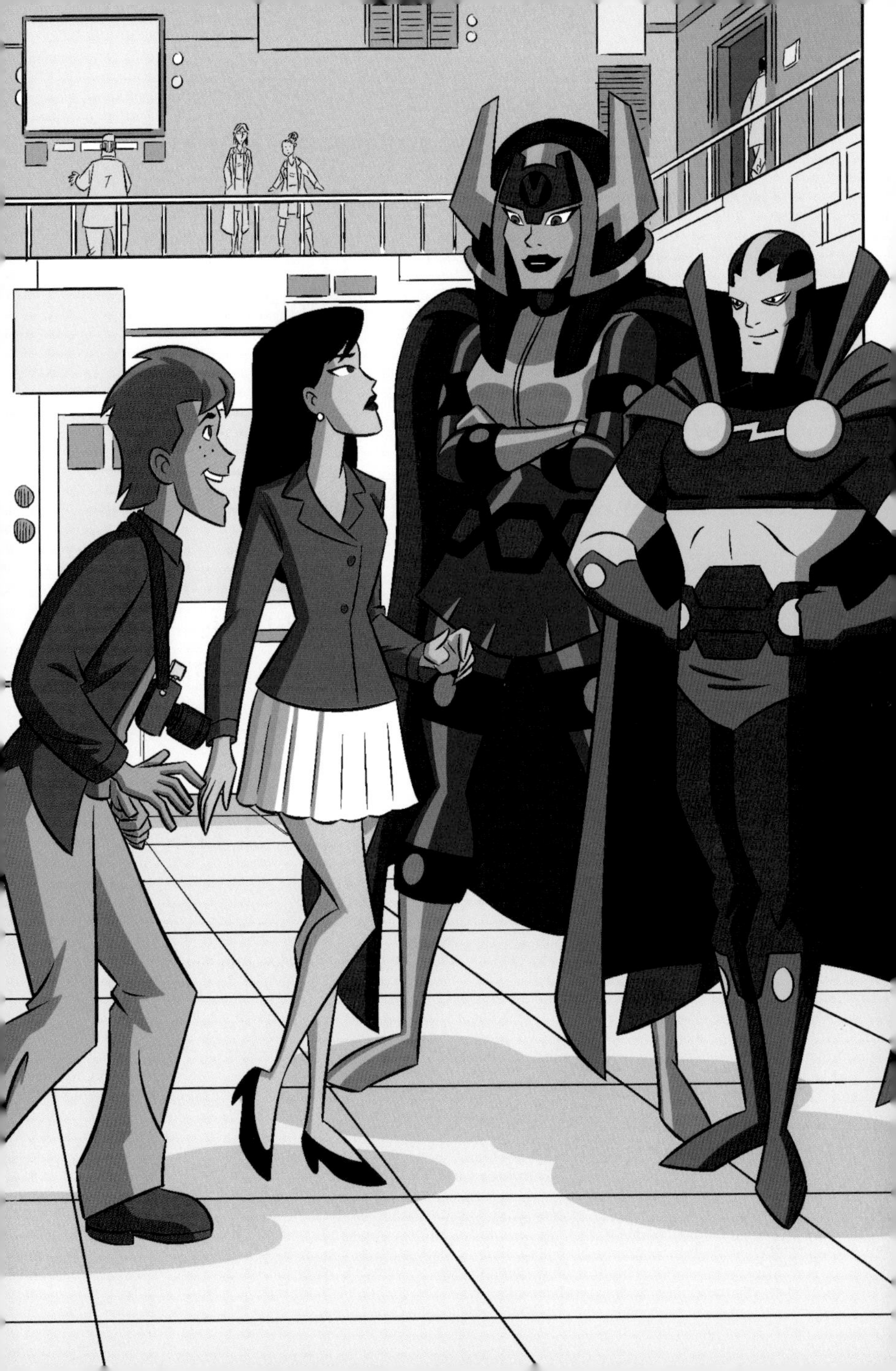

"Superman won't be coming back any time soon," Mister Miracle said. "That Boom Tube led straight to Apokolips. I'm guessing it closed because Superman destroyed the device that opened it—"

"What are you saying?" Lois asked.

"There's no way for him to get back on his own," said Big Barda.

CHAPTER 2

COUNTERSTRIKE!

"That can't be!" Lois exclaimed.

"No way!" added Jimmy, "After all, Superman can fly through space!"

"I know," replied Mister Miracle, "but Apokolips is too far from Earth. Even at top speed it would take him *years* to return."

"Unless we can get him this," Big Barda said. She opened her left hand to reveal a glowing, rectangular device. Slightly bigger than a smartphone, it was covered with strange symbols and glowing lights.

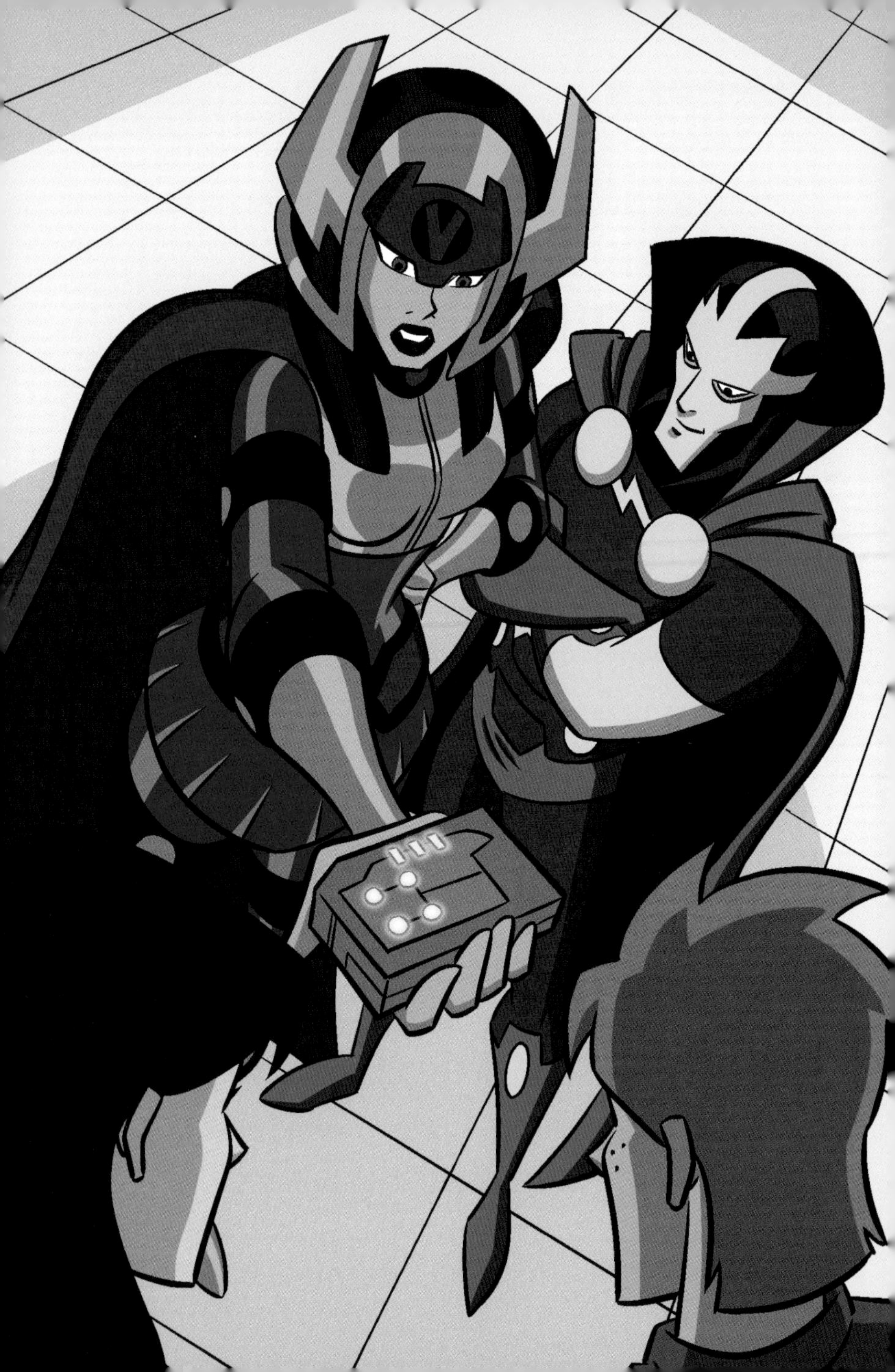

"This is a Mother Box," Big Barda said. "It can open a Boom Tube connecting Earth to Apokolips."

"Why do *you* have one?" asked Lois.

"Barda was born on Apokolips," replied Miracle. "She and I escaped that dreadful planet years ago."

"Were those creatures here to take you back?" asked Jimmy.

"This invasion has nothing to do with us," said Barda. "I think Apokolips's ruler, Darkseid, launched this Parademon invasion as a trap. By bringing Superman to his world, Earth is nearly defenseless against an even bigger attack."

"Why does Earth even matter to Darkseid?" Lois asked.

"Darkseid hates Earth because it shows the universe the power of free will," Mister Miracle answered. "We can live our lives the way we want to, but the people of Apokolips can't. Darkseid fears what would happen if his people learned about free will. If he defeats Earth, his grip on his people, and the universe, grows stronger!"

"But we won't let *that* happen," said Barda. "We'll head to Apokolips and bring Superman back before Darkseid attacks Earth again and—"

"No!" Lois exclaimed.

Big Barda raised an eyebrow. She wasn't used to being told no.

"I was trained as a Female Fury—one of Darkseid's greatest warriors—before I escaped his lieutenant, Granny Goodness," Barda replied. "You'd disagree with *my* strategy?"

"Let me explain," said Lois, taking a deep breath. "You and Mister Miracle know more about Darkseid than anyone currently on Earth. If he launches another attack before you return, we'll be helpless!"

"A fair point," replied Barda. "So what do you suggest?"

"Jimmy and I will go," Lois said.

"Um . . . Lois?" Jimmy's face went pale. He looked even more surprised than Barda and Miracle. "We're not exactly trained warriors."

"I know, Jimmy," Lois replied, "but we're reporters with war zone experience. And just imagine the photos you'll be able to take!"

Jimmy knew better than to argue with Lois when she had made a decision. "I guess you're right," he agreed, though he still looked worried.

"Give us a moment," Barda said as she pulled Miracle into a corner of the lab. After a short discussion, they returned.

"We have come to an agreement," said Barda.

"We'll give you the Mother Box," said Miracle. "But we're going to give you a crash course in using two of our weapons before you go. They may be your only chance of success."

"This is a Mega-Rod," said Barda, handing Lois her glowing, baton-shaped weapon. "It can fire powerful, tightly controlled bursts of energy. Give it a try."

Lois shifted the weapon from one hand to the other. Then she aimed the rod at a wastebasket.

KA-ZZAPPPPP!

The basket sailed across the room in one direction. Lois flew in the opposite direction!

"Sorry," said Big Barda, wincing a little. "I forgot to mention the recoil."

"I never would have guessed," said Lois as she got up and brushed herself off. "Let's try that again."

While Barda continued training Lois, Mister Miracle handed Jimmy a pair of shiny, thin metallic circles. Each one was about a foot across. As Jimmy took them, he began rising off the ground.

"What on earth?" Jimmy gasped.

"These are Aero Discs," said Miracle. "They allow you to fly at pretty high speeds, but you have to be—"

CRAAAAAAAASHHHHH!

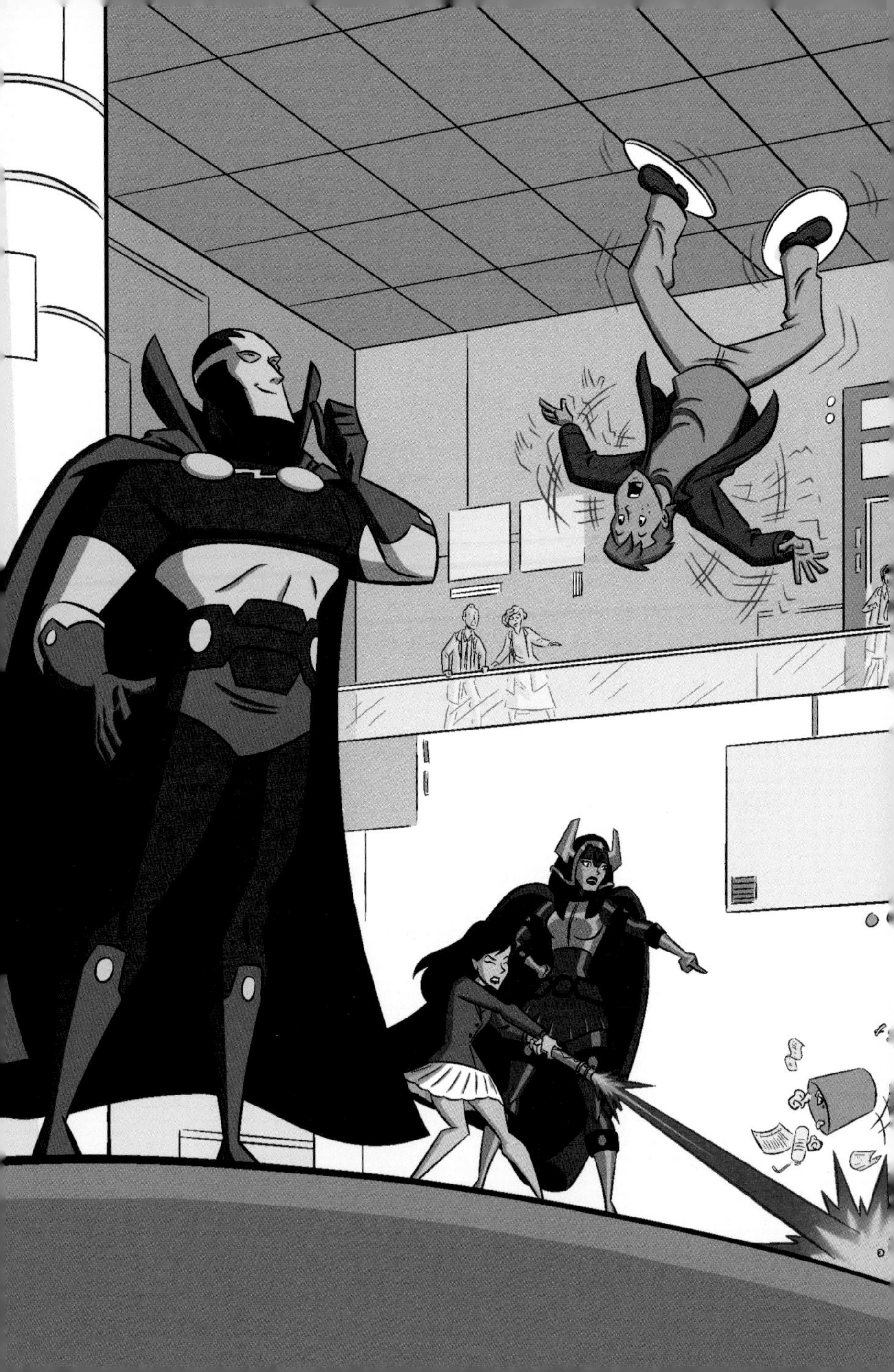

"—careful," said Mister Miracle, trying hard not to laugh.

"Noted!" Jimmy replied, now hanging upside down against the ceiling.

Mister Miracle reached up and pulled Jimmy down by his arm. Then he gave the photographer some pointers on how to control the discs.

After a couple of hours—and more than a few bruises—both Jimmy and Lois got the hang of their new gadgets. But time was running out.

"I don't think we can risk waiting any longer," said Mister Miracle. "Darkseid could launch another attack at any time. And he and his lieutenants on Apokolips may be giving Superman a pretty serious challenge as we speak."

Barda handed Lois the Mother Box and showed her how to turn it on. Lois rested her fingers on some of the symbols on the box's surface. With a few quick motions, the box sprang to life.

PING! PING! PING! PING! PING!

A cylinder-shaped Boom Tube formed in front of them.

"Remember," Barda shouted over the pinging noise, "watch out for the Female Furies! I trained you as well as I could in an *afternoon*. But they've spent years learning from the same woman who taught *me*."

Lois and Jimmy nodded as they stepped into the tube.

BOOOOMMMMMMM!

The tube vanished, taking Lois and Jimmy along with it.

CHAPTER 3

TO THE RESCUE!

BOOOOOOOM!

Lois and Jimmy dropped out of the Boom Tube and landed in the middle of a war-torn street on Apokolips. A block away, they spotted a stout, white-haired woman giving orders to four other women.

As the women pointed their weapons at a group of citizens, Lois and Jimmy scrambled behind a pile of rubble. Jimmy began taking photos of the scene.

"That white-haired woman must be Granny Goodness," said Lois. "That makes those other women her Female Furies!"

"Big Barda's old school pals," joked Jimmy. "They look even tougher than she said. We'd better stay here until the fight eases up, right, Lois?"

"Lois?" Jimmy spun around and realized he was alone!

Looking through his camera's viewfinder, Jimmy spotted Lois heading toward the action. She dodged from one pile of rubble to the next, holding Barda's crackling Mega-Rod in her hand.

Oh no! Jimmy thought to himself in disbelief. *She's going to take on the Furies single-handed!*

"Fight on, my Furies," shouted Granny Goodness, "teach these 'lowlies' what happens when they disobey the mighty Darkseid!" The Fury in front raised her razor-sharp whip in the air.

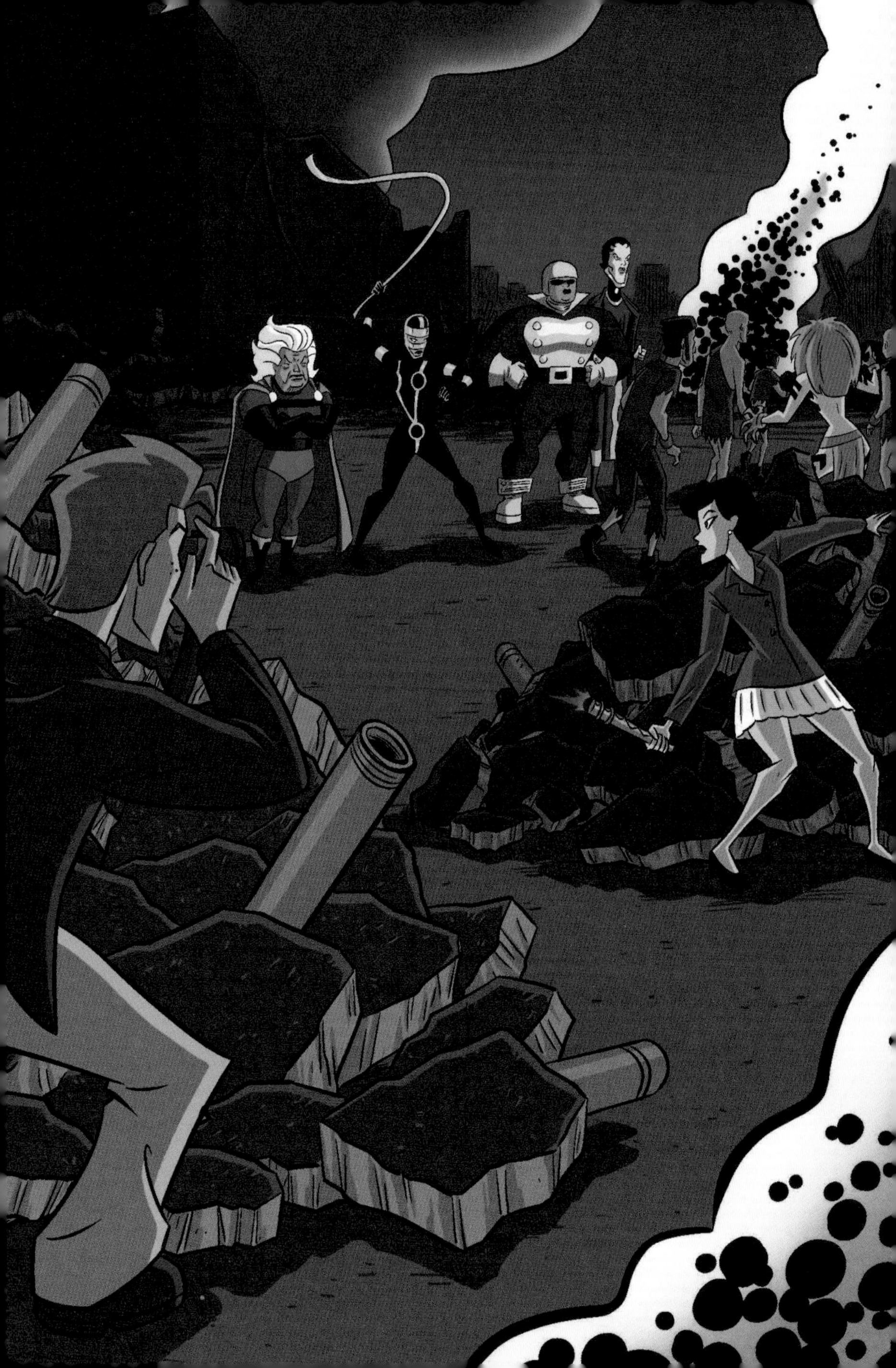

That must be Lashina, Lois thought as she peeked over a pile of rubble. *Big Barda mentioned her during my training. Those unarmed people don't have a chance against her and the Furies!*

Lashina's whip crackled with electricity as she swung it again.

KA-ZZAPPPPP!

Before Lashina's whip landed its blow, a Mega-Rod blast shredded it!

The crowd scattered as the Furies turned toward the source of the blast. They found Lois standing with the Mega-Rod firmly in hand, ready to fire again.

"I'm starting to get the hang of this weapon," Lois said. "So don't take another step, Furies, or I'll—"

GRRRMMMBBBLLL!

The ground quaked and rumbled as Stompa slammed down one of her powerful, high-tech boots. The shock wave rattled the war-torn buildings lining the street, causing several to collapse.

BOOM!

When the dust settled, huge mounds of rubble blocked the street. Moving quickly, Lois wedged herself into a tiny crack in the nearest mountain of debris. She knew she couldn't hide forever, but the longer she stayed out of the Furies' clutches, the better.

Moments later, Lois heard footsteps approaching. Through a crack in the rubble, she spied two Furies searching for her.

"Come out, come out, wherever you are," called Mad Harriet, raking her mechanical power claws against the rubble. "I have an itch I need to scratch!"

"Are you cold, dearie?" asked Bernadeth, waving her red-hot Fahren-Knife in the air. "I have something that can warm you up!"

HA! HA! HA! HA! HA!

The Furies' laughter sent a shiver down Lois's spine. Then the laughing stopped.

WHOOOSH!

"Did you see that?" Stompa asked. "Something red and blue just streaked overhead."

"Yes," replied Mad Harriet. "It must be the Kryptonian! Come! Let's find him. Granny Goodness will reward us if we bring him to mighty Darkseid!"

"Superman?" Lois wondered out loud. After a minute of silence, she crawled out of her hiding place.

"Lois! Run!" a voice called out behind her.

The reporter spun around to find Jimmy Olsen charging toward her in a panic. As he passed, she quickly matched his strides. Then she realized he was missing something.

"Jimmy, where are Mister Miracle's Aero Discs?" Lois asked.

"Well," Jimmy started to explain, "I saw you were in trouble, so I found some scraps of cloth and—"

K·CLANG!!!!!

"That wasn't Superman!" shouted Granny Goodness somewhere behind them. "You brought down a flying decoy! Find the Earth woman and bring her to me!"

"I hope Mister Miracle can get a new set of Aero Discs," Jimmy said. He glanced behind him and saw the Female Furies closing in fast.

"I think that's the least of our worries, Jimmy!" Lois shouted, grabbing the photographer's arm. "Look out!"

Jimmy and Lois skidded to a stop at the edge of one of Apokolips's Fire Pits. Sparks and smoke rose from the crater. It looked ready to erupt with cosmic fire at any moment.

WHOOSH!

A caped figure flew through the smoke. He grabbed Lois and Jimmy and soared into the air.

"Superman!" they both shouted.

As the Fire Pit sprayed energy into the sky, the Man of Steel carried them as far away as possible. But something was wrong. He quickly lost speed, and before long he had to return them to the ground.

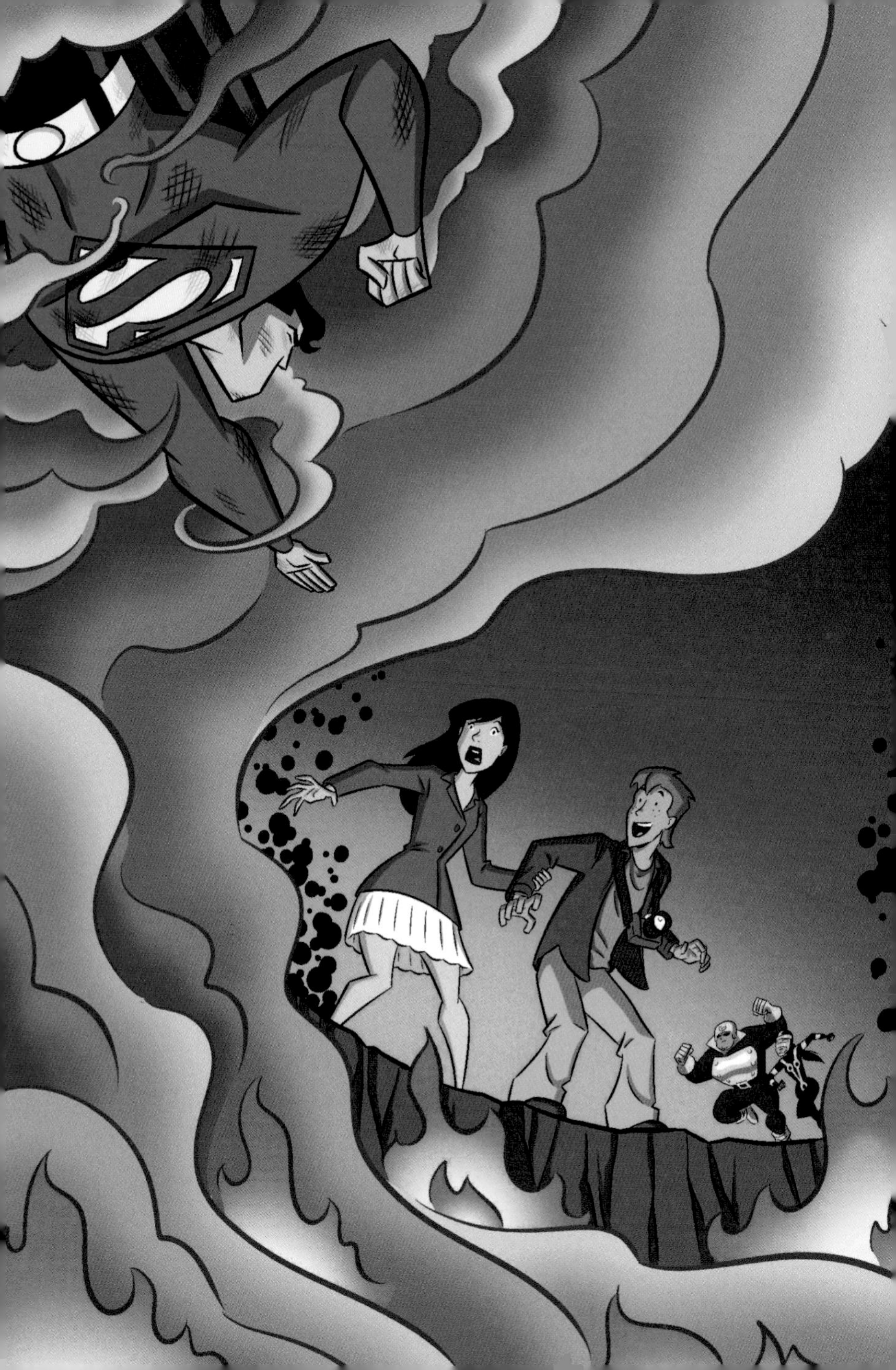

"I'm glad you two are all right," said Superman. He was covered in cuts and bruises, and he looked tired. "I spotted your fight with the Furies with what was left of my telescopic vision. I tried—"

"What do you mean, what was *left* of your vision?" Lois asked. "What's happened to your powers?"

"And your costume?" added Jimmy, noticing the Man of Steel's smudged and dusty uniform.

"I've been on the run from Darkseid's minions since I arrived," Superman said. "Even worse, Darkseid has somehow changed the environment of Apokolips. It's weakening my powers."

"If he can do that, why hasn't he attacked you already?" Lois asked.

"Darkseid has much bigger plans. He doesn't want to attack me in private," Superman answered. "He wants the people of Apokolips—the ones he calls 'lowlies'—to see him defeat me. He thinks watching me fall to him will break the spirit of their resistance movement once and for all."

Superman wiped his brow and gave his friends a tired smile. Then he noticed the Mega-Rod in Lois's hand.

"I was about to ask you two how you got here, but I see you are carrying Big Barda's Mega-Rod," Superman said. "She doesn't usually loan out her most prized weapons. Did you happen to talk her into giving you a Mother Box too?"

Lois nodded. She pulled the Mother Box out of her pocket and handed it to Superman.

It was instantly clear that Superman had used a Mother Box before. With the push of a few symbols, the device lit up. But this time it didn't open a Boom Tube.

PING! PING! PING! PING!

The Mother Box glowed brightly as Superman passed it over his body. It healed his wounds and even returned his uniform to normal!

"Aaaaaah! That's better," said Superman. "A Mother Box can't restore my powers completely, but it can help me feel more like myself again. Now it's time to take the fight to Darkseid!"

CHAPTER 4

ON THE ATTACK

"What's the plan, Superman?" asked Jimmy. "How can we help?"

"I'm afraid you can't, Jimmy," Superman said, giving his friend a thoughtful look. "In fact, I need to use the Mother Box to send you and Lois home."

"What?" said Lois. "We didn't come all this way just to leave you here. We're staying until you're ready to go back to Earth."

"That's very kind, Lois," explained Superman, "but Apokolips is too dangerous. Besides, I can't risk Darkseid using you two as hostages to force me to surrender."

"He makes a good point," Jimmy said. "Darkseid knows Superman would sacrifice himself before letting an innocent person get hurt."

"That may be," Lois answered. "But just because Darkseid thinks that's Superman's greatest weakness, doesn't mean *we* should treat it that way. Caring about regular people is Superman's greatest strength."

Lois turned to face Superman. "It's what makes you more than just a super hero. It makes you an inspiration—and I think we should use that to our advantage."

"You're right about one thing, Lois," Superman replied. "The people of Apokolips need to see someone stand up to Darkseid. If you two can stay out of sight and report what happens, maybe we can show *everyone* that Darkseid can be defeated."

"This is going to be the story of a lifetime," Lois said, smiling.

"Of course," added Superman, "this plan will depend on one thing."

"What's that?" Jimmy asked.

"For it to work," Lois replied, "Superman must actually *defeat* Darkseid."

* * *

A huge crowd gathered around the walls surrounding Darkseid's palace. Lois and Jimmy, now disguised as "lowlies," mingled unnoticed among the masses. They watched as Superman approached the wall with a look of determination. In his weakened state, they knew he would need to use his brains as well as his brawn.

The Man of Steel balled his fists and pounded on the wall's heavy, stone doors.

BOOM! BOOM! BOOM!

Superman's thunderous blows caused gasps from the crowd. But the impacts didn't even dent the doors.

"Darkseid!" Superman called out. "Would you care to step outside?"

Superman's challenge was met with silence.

Well, the polite approach didn't work, he thought. *No surprise. Bullies only like to fight on their OWN terms.*

Superman took a step back from the door and looked around. Then he urged the crowd to stand back.

Taking a running start, the hero used his full strength to strike the door.

KA-CHUNNNNNGGGGGG!!!!!!

The door split open, exploding into pieces that clattered into the palace courtyard.

That should attract some attention, Superman thought as he walked into the palace courtyard.

"You think you've earned the chance to face my father, Superman?" a gruff voice shouted. "Think again. You must get past *me* first!"

Kalibak, Darkseid's son, lumbered out of the courtyard's shadows. Although not as smart as Darkseid, Kalibak was a brutal fighter and a dangerous foe.

Darkseid must want Kalibak to wear me down before he faces me head-to-head, Superman thought. *I'll have to wrap this up fast!*

As Kalibak swung his enormous club, Superman dodged at dizzying speed.

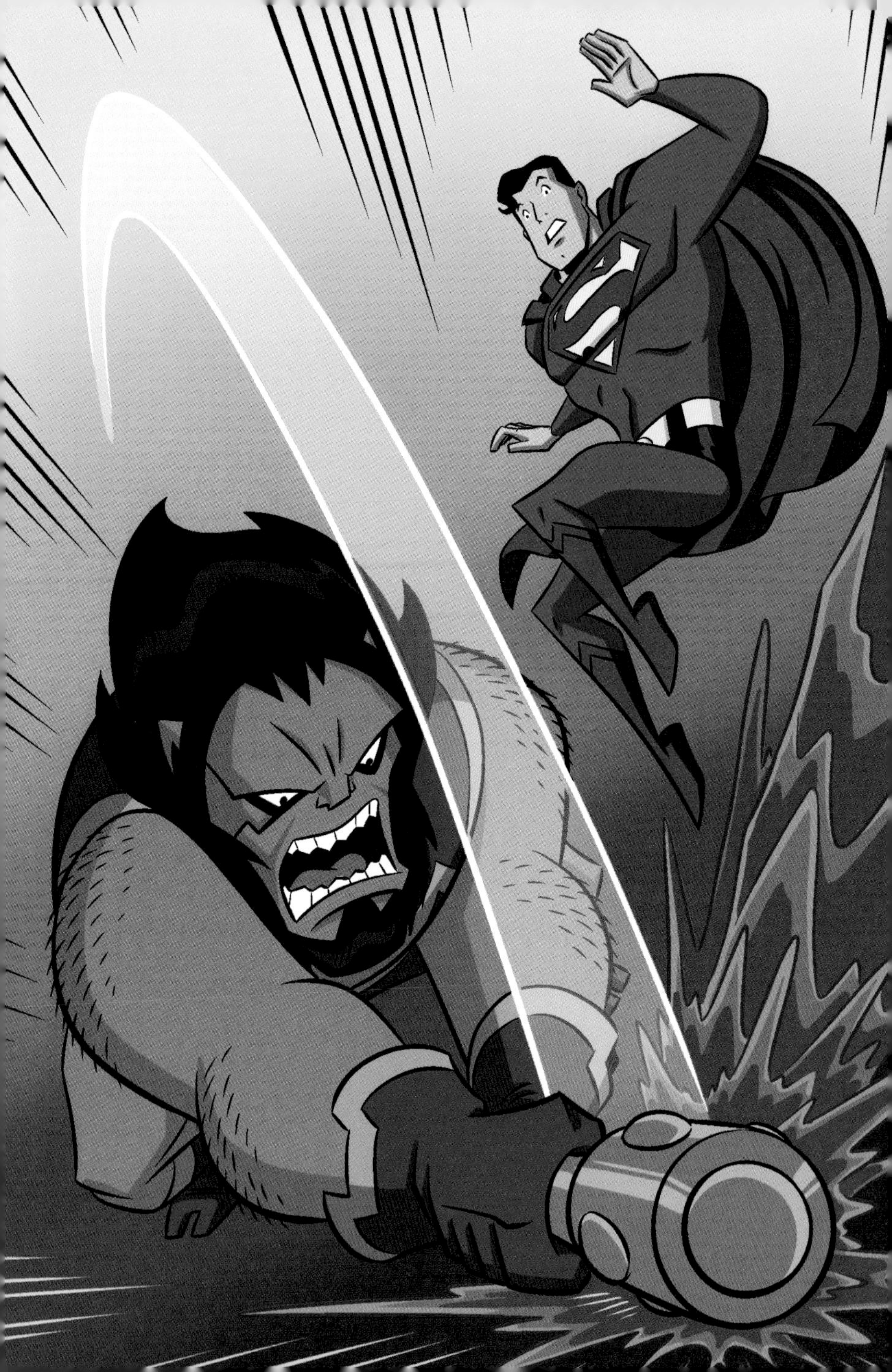

WHACK!

The club missed the hero and smashed a huge crater in the ground. A spray of filthy liquid exploded from the bottom of the crater.

Is that mud? Superman wondered, training his X-ray vision on the crater. Just beneath its surface he could see a massive sewer pipe. *No, it's definitely not mud—and that gives me an idea.*

Kalibak swung his club again. This time Superman stood still and caught the head of the club in his bare hands.

"Ooof!" the Man of Steel grunted as he pushed back on the huge weapon. Using every ounce of strength, he drove Kalibak into the crater! Then, with a blast of heat vision, he opened a large gap in the massive underground sewer pipe.

As Kalibak tried to rip his weapon free, Superman swept the villain's leg with his own. Knocked off-balance, Kalibak tumbled headfirst into the gap in the sewer pipe. The fast-moving current quickly carried the villain far from Darkseid's castle.

I wonder who Darkseid will send after me next? Superman thought as he walked deeper into the palace. He didn't have to wait long for an answer.

"Welcome, Kryptonian!" exclaimed a fancy-looking man slashing a sword through the air. "Care to face me in a duel?"

Superman recognized the man instantly. He now faced Kanto, Darkseid's weapons master. No one on Apokolips was more skilled with a sword. Luckily, Superman also knew that no one on Apokolips had a bigger ego.

"Swords aren't really my thing, Kanto. How about you fight me without weapons?" Superman replied. "Though I guess even my *weakened* powers are probably too much for you to overcome."

"Foolish Superman," Kanto replied, dropping his sword. "Have you forgotten that Kanto's *greatest* weapon is his skill in *all* forms of combat?"

Kanto leaped high in the air and delivered a flying kick to Superman's chest. The Man of Steel flew backward and skidded across the ground.

Superman struggled to his feet as Kanto circled him.

"I thought you'd put up more of a fight," Kanto said with a laugh. "But you're so weak you can't even fly away, can you?"

But, suddenly, Superman wasn't standing. He was *floating!*

"Oh, I can fly," the hero said as he hovered closer to Kanto. "I was just resting a little. I didn't want to waste my energy on the opening act."

"Opening act?!" roared Kanto, closing the gap between them.

"Maybe you don't have those on Apokolips. On Earth, it's what we call a minor attraction before the main show," said Superman as he raised his right hand. "And I should stress the word *minor.*"

Then Superman gave Kanto's forehead a flick.

SMAKKK!

The villain fell to the ground, knocked out with just one finger!

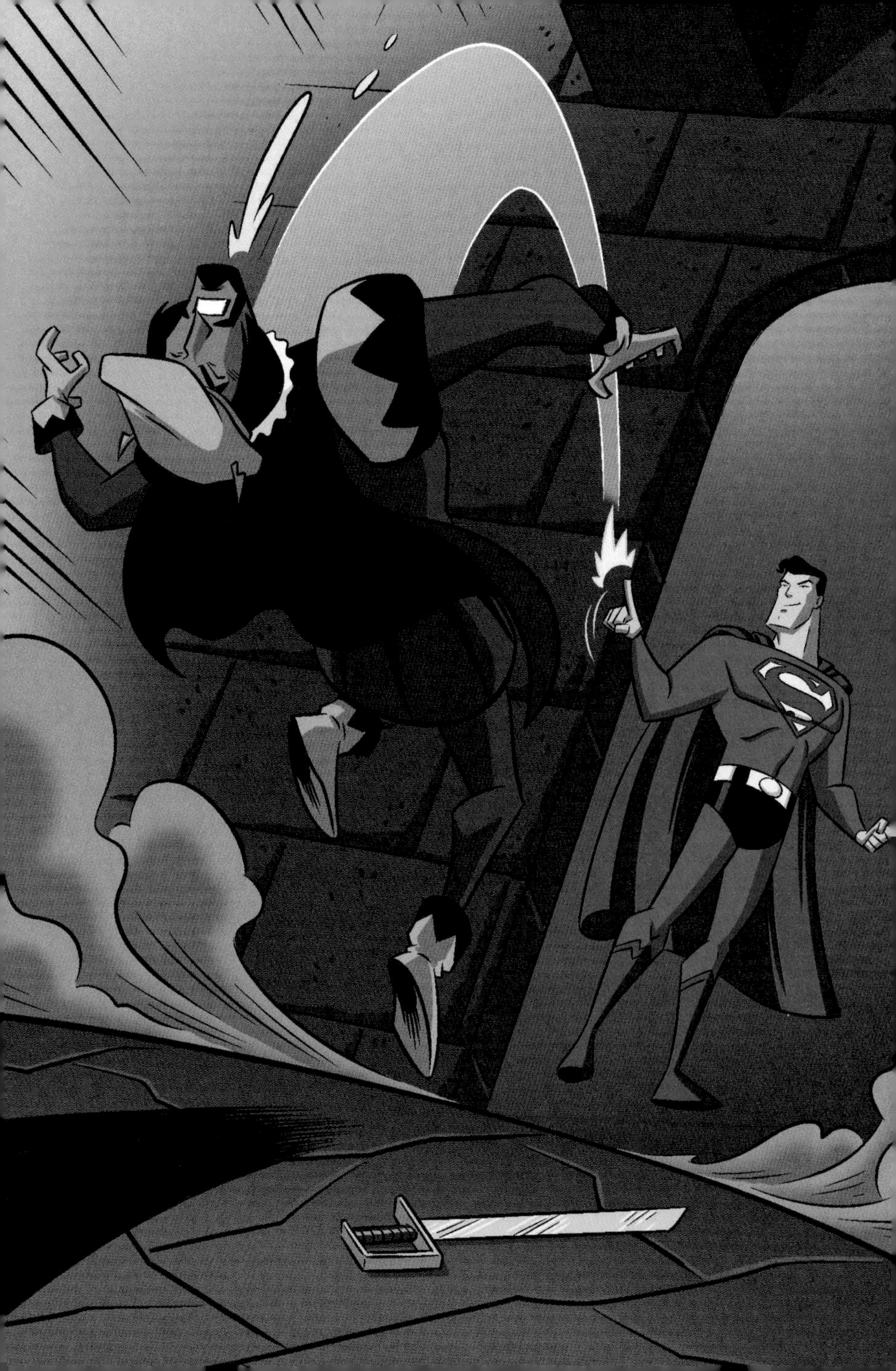

That was fun, thought Superman, *but I can't spend any more time on these minions. I have to take the fight to Darkseid—and fast!*

"Are you ready to face me yet, Darkseid?" Superman called out. "Or do you want to send more of your goons to do your dirty work for you?"

For a moment there was silence. Then a light shone from the depths of the palace.

TZZZZZZZZ!!!!

A pair of pure-white energy bolts curved toward Superman. They struck him head-on, and the Man of Steel disappeared without a trace!

CHAPTER 5

FACE-TO-FACE

FLASH!

Blinded by bright light for a moment, Superman worried that he had misjudged Darkseid. Maybe the villain thought winning from a distance was more important than crushing Superman in front of an audience.

But as Superman's eyes adjusted, he discovered he had been right all along. Darkseid's Omega Beams had brought him to the center of a vast arena. The weakened hero would battle the Lord of Apokolips in front of a massive crowd.

The arena was eerily silent. The lowlies in the crowd were afraid that any sound would be punished by Darkseid's Parademon enforcers. But they were also awed that a single man—even if he was Superman—was willing to battle their ruler alone.

"Welcome, Kryptonian," said Darkseid. He sat in a stone throne overlooking the arena floor. With his gray skin, the massive villain looked like a living statue. "I offer you one last chance to give up. Otherwise I shall end you while all of Apokolips cheers their ruler's ultimate triumph."

"That's a generous offer, Darkseid. But the people of Apokolips have waited long enough to see someone stand against you. And even if you've weakened my powers . . . ," Superman said, rising up and floating at eye level with Darkseid, "I. Still. Stand."

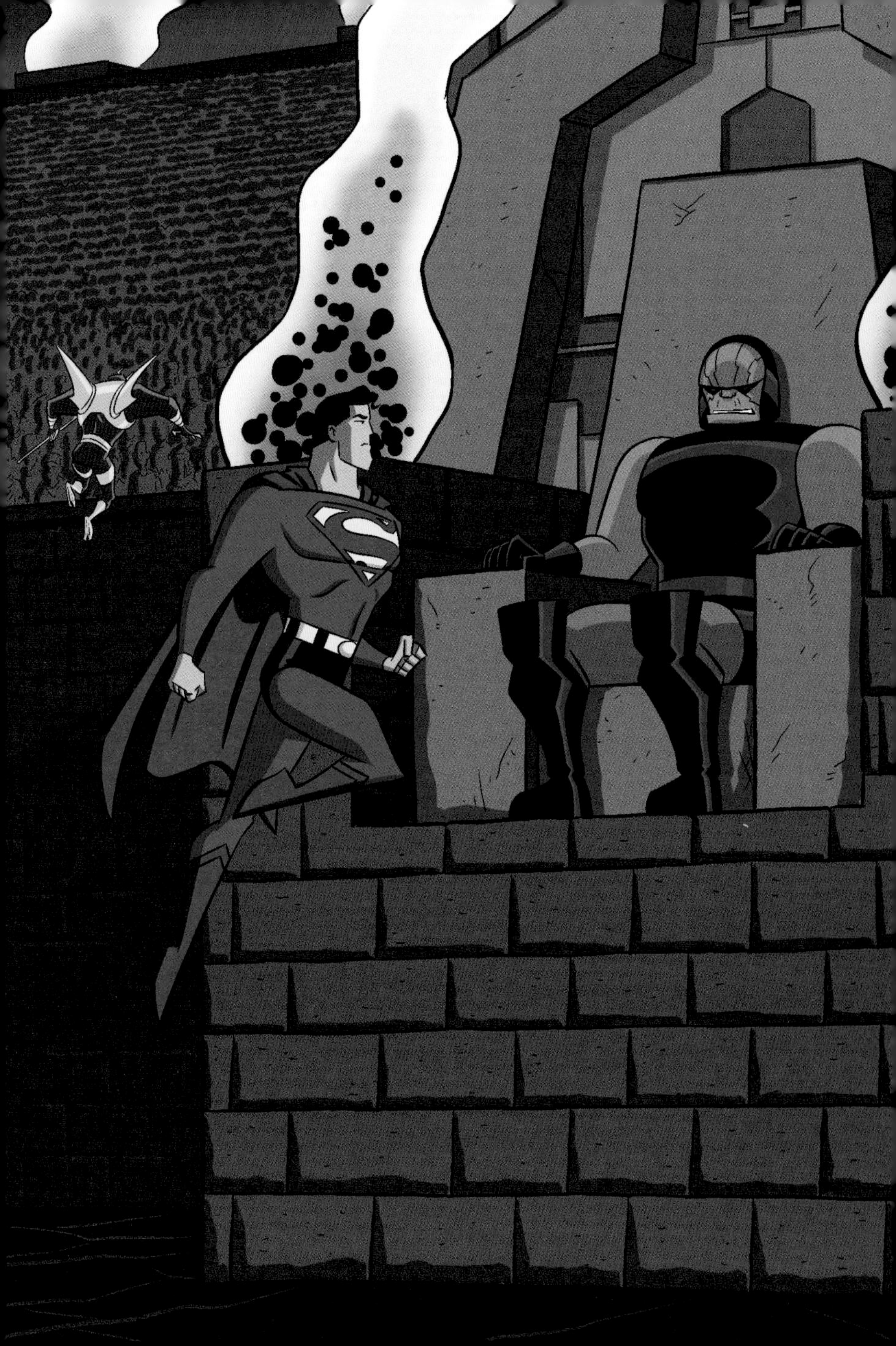

CLAP! The sound of a pair of hands coming together shattered the arena's silence.

CLAP-CLAP! Another pair of hands soon joined in.

CLAP-CLAP-CLAP! Suddenly the whole arena exploded in thunderous applause.

Darkseid's Parademons rose to silence the crowd. But with so many lowlies cheering and clapping, they didn't know whom to punish first.

K-ZAPPPPP! The crowd went silent as Darkseid fired an energy blast from one of his hands. It struck Superman, sending him skidding across the arena floor.

Darkseid leaped from his throne and landed in front of Superman. As the hero struggled to get up and catch his breath, Darkseid punched him in the stomach.

"Ooof!" said Superman, holding his stomach as he doubled over in pain. But instead of fighting back, he scanned the crowd with his telescopic vision. Within two heartbeats, he picked out Lois and Jimmy in the crowd.

Glad they're getting a good view, Superman thought as a slight smile crossed his face. *I just hope Jimmy's pictures don't make me look as bad as I feel.*

"Smiling, Superman?" asked Darkseid. "You'll have to tell me what you find so funny—after you recover from my fists!"

BAM! BAM! BAM! BAM!

Darkseid pummeled Superman, sending him sailing into the arena's wall.

I can't take too much more of this, thought Superman. *I have to find an advantage.*

As Darkseid lumbered toward him, Superman realized that, even weakened, he still had one thing Darkseid didn't—speed.

WHOOSH! In a blur of motion, Superman circled *behind* his foe. As Darkseid turned to face him, Superman's fist connected with Darkseid's jaw.

WHAM!

The punch sent Darkseid spinning like a top. Before the villain could find his footing, Superman leaped into the air. Then, with incredible force, he came down feet first and pounded Darkseid to the ground.

As Darkseid staggered to his feet, Superman caught him from behind in a bear hug. The hold pinned the villain's arms and kept him from facing Superman. As the Man of Steel squeezed, Darkseid's breathing slowed. Soon he would have to surrender.

The crowd rose to its feet. The lowlies looked on in stunned silence as they saw their ruler on the verge of defeat! Then a deep voice cut through the silence.

"Darkseid!" shouted Granny Goodness. "We have guests!"

Superman's heart sank. He knew what had happened even before he looked. Granny's Female Furies had captured Lois and Jimmy!

In the stands, Bernadeth held Lois's arm with one hand and her fiery blade with the other. With a quick blast of freezing-cold super-breath, Superman turned the blade brittle, and it shattered into tiny bits of ice!

But Mad Harriet stood behind Jimmy, snapping her mechanical claws menacingly. Superman wasn't sure he could stop her from hurting either of his friends from a distance.

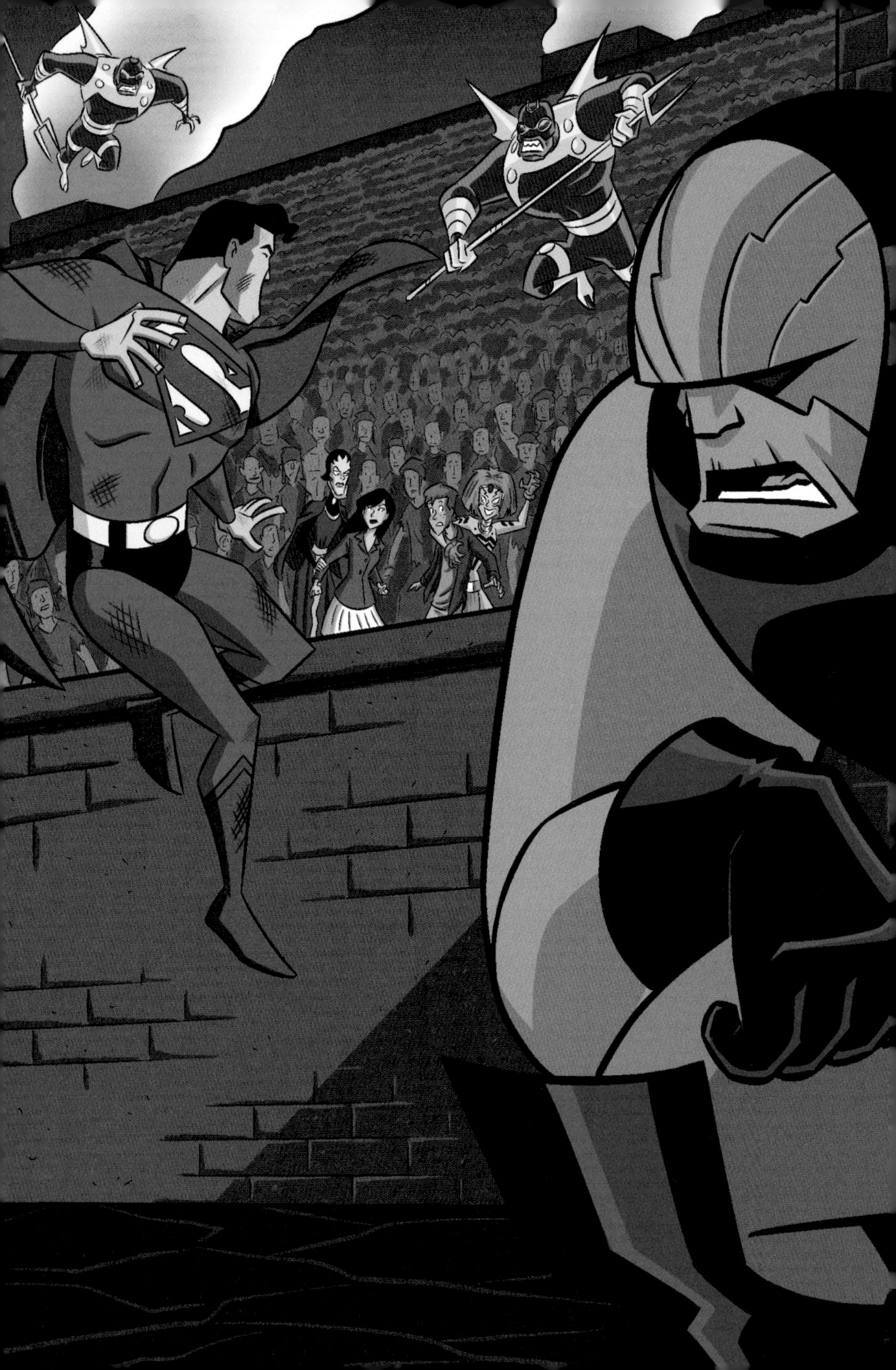

"Do you want to test your speed, Kryptonian?" taunted Harriet.

Superman couldn't risk Jimmy or Lois getting hurt. With no other choice, the hero released his hold on Darkseid. Still recovering from Superman's powerful grip, Darkseid staggered back to his throne.

"Your friends' attempt to help hasn't worked out, has it, Superman?" Darkseid said with a weak laugh. The villain looked tired as he leaned on the throne's armrests.

"But I can be generous," Darkseid continued. "Give up now, and I'll use my Omega Beams to send these two humans home to Earth. Refuse, and I'll sentence them to join you for a lifetime of hard labor with the lowlies!"

"Don't do it, Superman!" Jimmy shouted.

"Look at him," Lois added. "He's nearly beaten. He knows he's going to lose!"

All around the arena, lowlies began to grumble. They'd never seen anything like this. Two people from Earth—both without any special powers—were actually standing up to Darkseid!

As the grumbling grew louder, the Parademons struggled to maintain order. Then the crowd began throwing whatever was in their hands. A shower of debris clattered onto the arena floor.

Superman grinned as a new emotion darkened Darkseid's face. It was a look of *fear*.

GRRRR! Darkseid growled like a cornered animal, his eyes glowing bright white. As his Omega Beams shot out toward the Man of Steel, Superman knew he had to act fast.

The Man of Steel turned and flew into the stands at blinding speed. He managed to scoop Lois and Jimmy up just as the Omega beams struck, capturing all of them in a burst of light!

FLASH!

In an instant, Superman, Jimmy, and Lois found themselves in the sky above Metropolis. Superman flew them back to S.T.A.R. Labs, where they found Big Barda and Mister Miracle right where Jimmy and Lois had left them.

"Lois, Jimmy, Superman!" Mister Miracle exclaimed. "I'm so glad you made it back!"

"Not as glad as we are," Lois replied, handing Big Barda her Mega-Rod. "Have there been any more Boom Tube attacks while we were away?"

"Not a one," Barda replied, holstering her weapon. "But with Superman back, we'll be ready if there are."

"I don't think Darkseid wants to face Superman anytime soon," Lois said. "When Darkseid saw the lowlies turning against him, he sent Superman home. He was afraid of what would happen if they got any more inspiration."

"But that was Darkseid's mistake," said Superman. "It wasn't me standing up to him that was the inspiration."

Jimmy and Lois both did double takes.

"It wasn't?" Jimmy asked.

"No," Superman replied. "It was you and Lois. If just two people without any powers could stand up to Darkseid—"

"Imagine how fast he'd run if *thousands* of people did," Lois finished.

"I bet Darkseid and his minions are running from an angry mob even as we speak," Superman continued. "Bullies can't handle it when people fight back."

"And that story is true on any planet," Lois said with a smile.

Darkseid

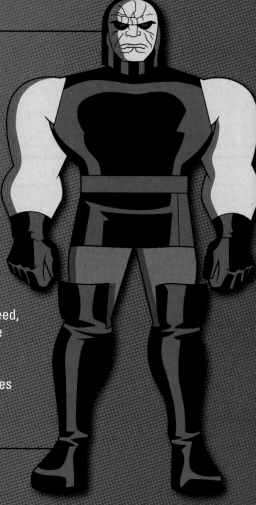

REAL NAME: Uxas

OCCUPATION: Dictator

BASE: Apokolips

HEIGHT: 8 feet, 9 inches

WEIGHT: 1,815 lbs.

EYES: Red

HAIR: None

POWERS/ABILITIES:
Superhuman strength, speed,
stamina, and durability. He
also has the power to fire
Omega Beams from his
eyes to teleport his enemies
anywhere he chooses.

BIOGRAPHY:

Uxas was the son of the King and Queen of Apokolips and was second in line to the throne. When he came of age, he killed his older brother, Drax, claiming the throne for himself—as well as the fabled Omega Force. The incredible object transformed Uxas into a rocklike creature, making him nearly resistant to harm. Now, as Darkseid, he rules Apokolips with an iron fist and aims to take down Superman, his only true threat.

- Darkseid is nearly invulnerable. However, incredible physical force, like a punch from the Man of Steel himself, can weaken or even injure Darkseid.

- As one of the New Gods, Darkseid's body is not subject to disease or aging. He is considered by most to be immortal.

- Injuring Darkseid is difficult enough, but even when he is actually hurt, he's capable of regenerating his body at an incredible pace.

- Darkseid uses his super-strength and endurance to wear down his opponents in battle. He can also shoot Omega Beams, or laser-like blasts, from his eyes (this ability is quite similar to Superman's heat vision).

BIOGRAPHIES

Author

Ivan Cohen has written comics, children's books, and TV shows featuring some of the world's most popular characters, including Teen Titans Go!, Batman, Spider-Man, Wonder Woman, Superman, the Justice League, and the Avengers. Ivan looks forward to reading this book to his wife and son in their home in New York City.

Illustrator

Cartoonist **Gregg Schigiel** is the creator/author/illustrator of the superhero/fairy tale mash-up *Pix* graphic novels and was a regular contributor to Spongebob Comics. Outside of work, Gregg bakes prize-winning cookies, enjoys comedy, and makes sure he drinks plenty of water. Learn more at greggschigiel.com.

GLOSSARY

cosmic (KOZ-mik)—having to do with outer space, the universe, or the heavens

decoy (DEE-koi)—a person or object that draws someone's attention away from something

inspiration (in-spihr-AY-shun)—something that fills someone with an emotion, an idea, or an attitude

invulnerable (in-VUHL-nur-uh-buhl)—unable to be harmed

lieutenant (loo-TEN-uhnt)—an officer of low rank in the military

mechanical (muh-KAN-uh-kuhl)—having to do with machines or tools

recoil (REE-koil)—the kickback of a gun when firing

resistance movement (ri-ZISS-tuhnss MOOV-muhnt)— a group of people that fights against an enemy that has taken control of the area

telescopic vision (TEL-uh-SKOP-ik VIZH-uhn)—the ability to see distant objects and make them seem larger and closer

X-ray vision (EKS-ray VIZH-uhn)—the ability to see inside a person or through objects

DISCUSSION QUESTIONS

1. Lois and Jimmy use a Mother Box to create a Boom Tube that takes them to Apokolips. If you had a Mother Box, where would you have a Boom Tube take you? Explain why you would like to go there.

2. Why does Darkseid send Superman, Lois, and Jimmy back to Earth at the end of the story? What is he afraid will happen if they stay on Apokolips any longer?

3. Lois and Jimmy went to Apokolips to help Superman and bring him home. Do you think the Man of Steel needed their help? Could he have defeated Darkseid on his own? Explain why you think so.

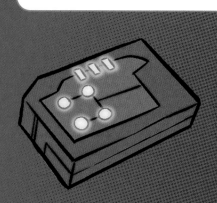